jumelle tout en cuir noir chagriné 1re qua-
grand cadre à charnières avec forte serrure nic-
à poussoir et à clé et 2 verrous automatiques,
res sellerie, fortes courroies cuir faisant le tour,
poignées en cuir articulées, intérieur doublé
toile avec séparation et poche. Modèle très ro-
. Recommandé.
dèle courant, long. 60 c/m, poids 4 kg 400. 35. »
Grand modèle, — 65 c/m, — 5 kg.... 38. »

jumelle en vache extra havane clair ou foncé,
d cadre à charnières avec forte serrure nickelée,
ussoir et à clé et 2 verrous automatiques, pi-

Nota. — Pour les housses en toile, porte-étiquette

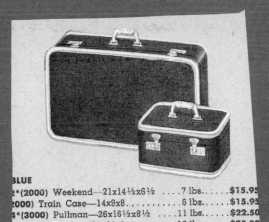

BLUE
*(2000) Weekend—21x14½x6½ ....7 lbs.....$15.95
2000) Train Case—14x9x8 ....6 lbs.....$15.95
(3000) Pullman—26x16½x8½ ....11 lbs.....$22.50
3600) Wardrobe—21x18x8 ....13 lbs.....$25.00

285. Sac à fond brisé en peau de porc naturelle
extra, cadre à charnières avec forte serrure nickelée
à poussoir et à clé et 2 forts crochets nickelés à bascule, piqûres sellerie renforcées, fortes courroies
cuir faisant le tour et poignée cuir articulée, intérieur doublé toile mastic extra fine avec 2 grandes
poches, long. 55 c/m, poids 4 kg. Fabrication
hors ligne................................... 65. »

à poussoir et à clé et 2
bascule, piqûres sellerie renforcées, fortes courroies
cuir faisant le tour et poignée cuir articulée, intérieur doublé toile mastic extra fine avec 2 grandes
poches,
hors ligne

SACS DE VOYAGE DITS " DE NUIT "

Genuine Alligator Club Bags.

No. 33Y5234
You have per-
haps read of such
things in irre-
sponsible adver-
tisements, but we
doubt if you ever
bought a genuine
Alligator Bag at
this low figure,
$3.25. Leath-
er lined, hinge stay.   Very handsome bag for
ladies' use. Your highest expectations realized.
Lgth. Wgt.   Price | Lgth. Wgt.   Price
12 in. 2½ lbs. $3.25 | 16 in. 3½ lbs. $4.25
14 in. 3 lbs. 3.75

Enameled Iron Covered Trunks.

B 3439 Extra
Heavy Iron En-
ameled Trunk;
large box, with
heavy iron cen-
ter band and
binding, two sole
leather straps,
brass-plated
steel clamps and
trimmings,large
monitor lock,
extra heavy side
bolts, sliding
leather handles,
steel hinges,
cloth faced tray
with two com-
partments sep-
arately covered. This is a very strong, serviceable trunk;
the slats are hardwood finished and run full length of trunk.

Size.	Weight.	Each.	Size.	Weight.	Each.
20 in.	40 lb.	$5.65	36 in.	55 lb.	$6.85
				65 lb.	7.25

UEUR CENTEN

et ont cet autre avantage, une fois vides, de
être roulées complètement de façon a ne plus forme
qu'un paquet de la grosseur du bras.

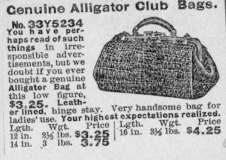

365. Valise pliante dite " Enveloppe de
voyage ", tout en toile tannée, poignée et cour
roies cuir faisant le tour, 2 grandes poches inté
poche extérieure à soufflet,dimension

: 21   Shipping w

AL605*(1560) — 2
AL604*(1920) — 2
AL605*(2400)

et the high class, correct, most up to
by some for old-style and inferior

B 3467—Combination Oxford and Suit Case,
made of very best hand-grained leather in rich
brown, large Oxford Bag on top, and a practi-
cal Suit Case on bottom; heavy imported frame
and stitched, leather

at left, from $25.00.* Also,
family ensembles in rich
genuine leather"Wheari-
lite". Prices (leather)
from $50.00*

RACINE WISCONSIN

18 in. long, weight, 6 lb. ....
20 in. long, weight, 7½ lb. ....
22 in. long, weight, 9 lb. ....

B 34
C a n
"Glad
Trav
Bag; n
drab
duck,
out s
straps
el loc
ners,
with g
le a t
cloth
will o

a leather satchel. 14 in., weight, 3
Each
16 in., weight, 4 lb. Each

Ask your dealer for them. Send for Booklet.
Stamped on bottom
WITHDRAWN

HH
JJ   KK

VOYAGE POUR

420. Sac de voyage pour
tout en vache vernie noire,
à charnière renforcé avec serrure,
ront nickelé, poignée cuir articulée. poche extérieure portefeuille
intérieur doublé fine peau avec
poche, long. 30 c/m, poids 520 gr.

PAGE 335 ... LUGGAGE

For Oli, Harry, and Claire

A Neal Porter Book
Published by Roaring Brook Press
Roaring Brook Press is a division of Holtzbrinck Publishing Holdings Limited Partnership
175 Fifth Avenue, New York, New York 10010

mackids.com

Library of Congress Cataloging-in-Publication Data

Names: Gordon, Gus, 1971– author, illustrator.
Title: Somewhere else / by Gus Gordon.
Description: First edition. | New York : Roaring Brook Press, 2017. | "A Neal
   Porter Book." | Summary: While other birds are seeing the world, George
   the duck is content to stay at home—or so it seems until he confesses the
   truth to Pascal, a visiting bear.
Identifiers: LCCN 2016058283 | ISBN 9781626723498 (hardcover)
Subjects: | CYAC: Travel—Fiction. | Flight—Fiction. | Ducks—Fiction. |
   Bears—Fiction. | Birds—Fiction.
Classification: LCC PZ7.G6573 Som 2017 | DDC [E]—dc23
LC record available at https://lccn.loc.gov/2016058283

Our books may be purchased in bulk for promotional, educational, or business use.
Please contact your local bookseller or the Macmillan Corporate and Premium Sales Department
at (800) 221-7945 ext. 5442 or by e-mail at MacmillanSpecialMarkets@macmillan.com.

The illustrations for this book were created using watercolor,
pencil, crayon, and lots of beautiful paper (old & new).

First edition 2017
Book design by Gus Gordon

Printed in China by RR Donnelley Asia Printing Solutions Ltd., Dongguan City, Guangdong Province

1 3 5 7 9 10 8 6 4 2

SOMEWHERE ELSE

gus gordon

A Neal Porter Book
Roaring Brook Press
New York

Some birds fly north.

Some birds fly south.

53.

héron

oie

drôle d'oiseau

Some birds take the bus.

Most birds go somewhere.

George Laurent wasn't like most birds.

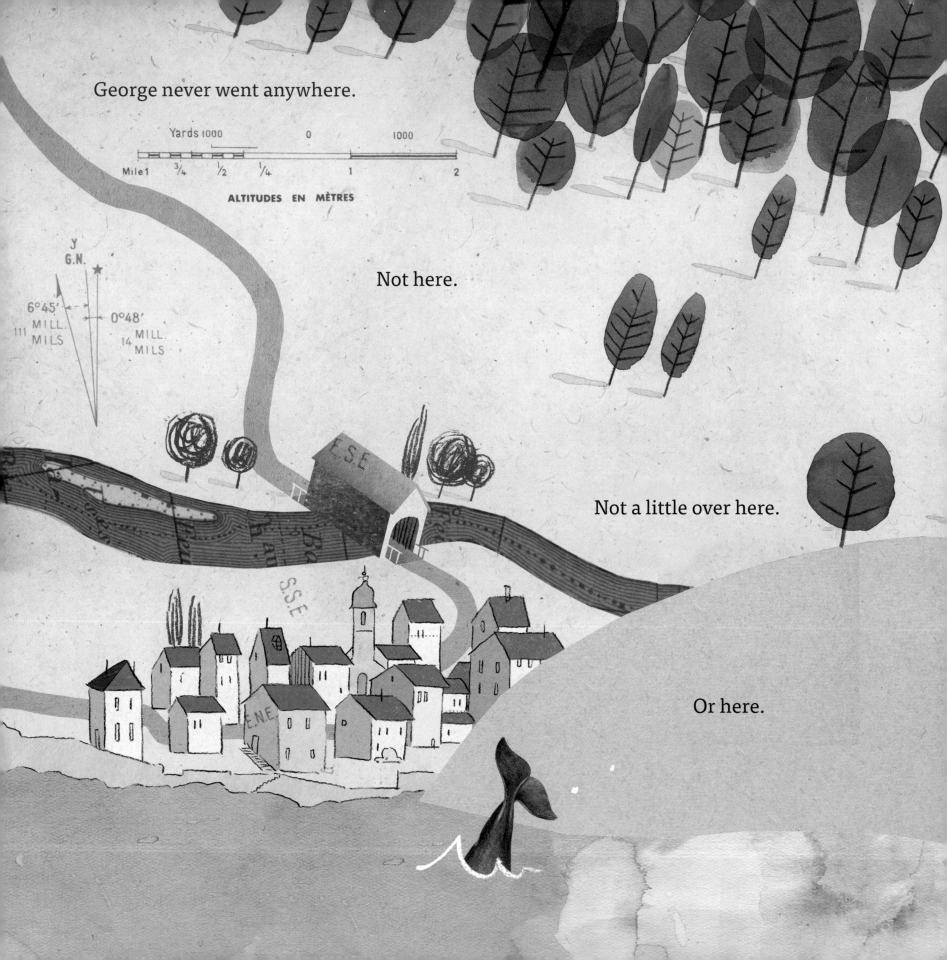

George never went anywhere.

Not here.

Not a little over here.

Or here.

Not even here!

Patiss-erie

Not anywhere.

"I like it here better than anywhere somewhere else," he told himself. Besides, there was always something nice baking in the oven.

N

NNW

E.

ANISETTE
TRI

George Laurent had a gift for baking the most astonishing pastries. Friends were always dropping by on their way to somewhere else.

One morning, Penelope Thornwhistle declared, "This éclair is almost as spectacular as soaring high above a sunrise in the Andes. Let's fly there together, George. It will be a hoot!"

But George wasn't interested.
He always had an excuse.
"Not today, Penelope. I've got brownies in the oven. I think this batch will win awards!"

The following afternoon,
Walter Greenburg popped in for
some delectable apple strudel.

"This apple strudel makes me think
of Paris at night, dear boy.
Come see it with me, George.
It's truly extraordinaire!"

"So sorry, Walter," said George. "I'd love to come but I've got a mountain of ironing to do."

The very next week, a flock of friends swooped in to sample some of George's prize-winning carrot cake.

"Have you seen the Alaskan tundra in the fall?" they cried. "It's like this cake—there are no words to describe its beauty!"

"How about WHOA?!!" someone suggested.

WHOA! wasn't enough.
George was going nowhere.
"Sorry, I've got a yoga class that day," he said.

As the seasons passed by, everyone stopped asking
George if he wanted to go somewhere else with them.
He was far too busy, it seemed.

Winter arrived and George found himself alone . . .

. . . except for Pascal Lombard.

Pascal was searching for a warm place to spend the winter.

"I wish I could fly, George," he said. "I hear the Caribbean is nice this time of year. Why aren't you somewhere else, on a beach in the sun?"

"I've been busy learning Flamenco songs on my guitar," said George.

"But you don't own a guitar, George," said Pascal.

"Actually, I've been watching the complete series of *Lost in Space*," said George.

"But you don't have a television," said Pascal.

"Well, in truth, I've been writing my memoirs," said George.

...and it was the yummiest blackberry pie I ever baked, on a Tuesday.

THE END

tap
tap
tap

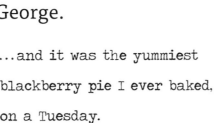

"But you're only five," said Pascal. "You haven't done anything yet!"

"Well, I would've gone somewhere else," said George . . .

"if only I knew how to fly."

George told Pascal how on that important day when everyone had learned to fly, he was simply doing something else.

He had been making excuses not to fly, ever since.

It just so happened that Pascal Lombard had an uncanny knack for solving tricky problems.

"George, I have an uncanny knack for solving tricky problems!" he announced. "We are going to teach you how to fly!"

They wasted no time.

First, they read some helpful books.

That didn't work out so well.

Then they got creative.

That didn't go so well either.

Then they ran out of good ideas. ➡

It turned out Pascal Lombard didn't have much of a knack for solving tricky problems after all.

"I don't think I was meant to fly," said George, sadly.
"I'll always be a stay-at-home kind of guy."
George felt disappointed. Pascal felt disappointed.
They spent the afternoon quietly reading by the fire.

Just as Pascal thought maybe it was time to go,
George pointed to Pascal's newspaper.
"What is that wonderful bubble thing?" he said.

LE BALLON

BULLETIN TRIMESTRIEL DE TOUTES LES ASCENSIONS

6me ANNÉE

Janvier, Février, Mars 1883

Un Numéro: 75 Centimes

Pour tous les Etats compris dans l'Union Générale des Postes.

RÉDACTION ET BUREAUX

A. BRISSONNET, Propriétaire Gérant

127, Boulevard Sébastopol.

PARIS

E. PICHOT, IMPRIMEUR.   72, QUAI JEMMAPES, PARIS.

It just so happened that Pascal Lombard was
remarkably good with his hands.
"George, I am remarkably good with my hands!"
he announced. "We can build it!"

And so they did.

It took all winter (it turned out Pascal Lombard
wasn't actually very good with his hands).

Finally, after some hiccups . . .

"We are flying, Pascal!" said George.
"Yes, we are, George," said Pascal. "Where shall we go?"
"I have some ideas," smiled George.

They traveled to all the places they had heard about and some they hadn't. "Paris at night really is extraordinaire!" said George.

Arctic Circle

George and Pascal flew for months.
The world was bigger and more
exciting than they had ever imagined.

But something was missing.

George's homemade pie.

"Where shall we go next winter?" said Pascal.
"Anywhere somewhere else," said George.

dées cuir, 2 étuis à parapluies, 1 étui à canne et u
poche extérieure à soufflet, avec bordure cuir, di
ouverte 122 × 70 c/m, poids 1 kg. 600. *Modèle inusab*
Recommandé..... 25. »

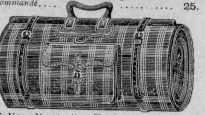

380. Valise pliante dite "**Enveloppe de voyage**"
tout en tissu tartan extra fort, doublée toile tannée
imperméable et bordée cuir, solide poignée et cour-

④ **hentic Wallace Red R**
Rayon with Black T

ay more Americans on the go are traveling
, smart and economical Atlantic lightwei
s hang wrinkle-free in your **VAL-A-PAK,**
obe. There is a **Grasshopper** for all accesso
f your trip. The **Hat Box** or **Train Case**

vide, est entièrement plat et son volume n'aug
s sacs sont très robustes et d'une extrême légèret

FISHER'S
GLADSTONE BAG
188, STRAND

Nota. — En dehors des articles du présen

lise jumelle en vache extra havane clair ou foncé,
rand cadre à charnières avec forte serrure nickelée.
poussoir et à clé et 2 verrous automatiques, pi

Nota. — *Pour les housses en toile, porte-étiu*

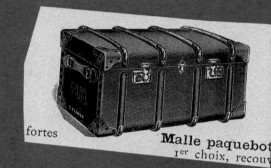

fortes

Malle paquebot
1er choix, recouv

Our High Grade, Leather Lined
English Traveling Bags.

No. 33Y5239 Eng-
lish Bag, extra high
and wide, heavy steel
frame, leath-
er covered,
hand stitch-
ed, best lock
and trim
mings. Eng-
lish auto-
matic catch-
es and inside
stay to hold
bag open.
English sunk
lock. A bag
especially
adapted for gentlemen's or ladies' use. Leather
lined, with three inside pockets. Colors, light
tan or dark brown.

Lgth.	Wgt.	Price	Lgth.	Wgt.	Price
14 in.	4¾ lbs.	$7.50	17 in.	5 lbs.	$9.00

22 inches, weight, 6 lb............
24 inches, weight, 6½ lb............ 3.30
                    7½ lb............ 3.65
                                   4.00

B 3482—New London Suit Bag. The latest
bag out; made of the best selected full stock
grain leather, sides and gussets, stiffened heavy
frame, with bottom shoes; corner catches and

med tygfoder, utan mellanskifte, men med
tvenne fickor inuti.

N:o 1007.

MAIN DE DAMES
à main pour dames. Ceux que nous présenton
mieux étudiés, d'un goût très sûr et pratique

entièrement
kelé, se ferma
par un petit
kelé à pouss
poche sur le
rabat et ferm
intérieur do
fin, nuance
poche, patte
également
grenat avec
et boucle
long. 12 c/m

485. Petit sac à main à
large soufflet, tout en peau
de phoque véritable noir
495A. La mèr

PLE-SEC

ivre, poignées et courroies cuir, interieur dou
ile avec une séparation et une poche moles-
Prix exceptionnel.
odèle courant, long. 60c/m. Poids 2 kg. 5. »
rand modèle, — 65c/m. — 2 kg.200. 5.50

mbée recouverte en toile tannée marron
é, coins protecteurs en cuir avec solides
ros clous et serrure cuivre, poignées et

The "LIKLY" No. 300 TRUNK
The latest product of the "Likly" factories.
Constructed upon an entirely new principle, in-
volving a unique method of interior re-inforcing
which guarantees great strength

Poids 2 kg. 300 ... 35 »
— 2 kg. 700 ... 38 »
— 3 kg. .... 41 »

tout en vache de qualité extra, couleur
noir métallique articulé et renforcé
carré, serrure cuivre à poussoir et à
rrous à bascule, piqûres sellerie, solide
articulée, intérieur doublé fine toile
de poche. *Modèle inusable et de grand cachet*